A REMINDER IN MY BACKPACK

WRITTEN AND ILLUSTRATED BY
ROB TOMAT

DEDICATION

This book is dedicated to my wife, Daniela, and my granddaughters, Avery and Lyla

A REMINDER IN MY BACKPACK

The end of summer was approaching. Soon it would be September, and Avery was so excited to be starting kindergarten. Her teacher would be Miss Paletta.

"I can just tell already that she will be a kind and fun teacher," said Avery to her parents. "I am also going to make lots of friends and learn really cool stuff. And now that I'm a big kindergarten girl, I will be able to climb to the top of the climber in the playground."

Avery's mom and dad smiled and told her they were so glad she was looking forward to starting school.

Just then, there was a knock at the door. It was Avery's grandfather, Papa.

"Hi Papa! I didn't know you were coming to see me today," Avery said as she greeted him with a big squishy hug.

Papa picked her up and gave her a kiss on the cheek. "I'm just stopping by on my way to the arena. Hockey registration is starting for the upcoming season and I want to make sure I get on a team. The goalie positions fill up very quickly."

Papa stayed for a few minutes and listened to Avery tell him about the exciting news of her upcoming season in kindergarten and all the thrilling things she had planned, including what she was going to wear on the first day.

The Labour Day weekend had arrived, and Avery and her parents went to Papa's house for one last barbeque of the summer.

Papa noticed that Avery didn't greet him with her usual big squishy hug. She seemed to be in deep thought.

"Is everything ok?" Papa asked Avery's mom.

"She has been very quiet all day today," replied Avery's mom. "We figured she would be so hyped up for school starting tomorrow," added Avery's dad.

As everyone was having dinner in the backyard, Avery sat on a stool off in a corner and wasn't eating much of her hamburger.

Papa noticed this and sat down beside her. They sat in silence for a couple of minutes before Papa spoke in a soft, quiet tone.

"What's going on in that little head of yours? Tell Papa what is on your mind."

Avery looked up at Papa with a very serious look on her face.

"Oh Papa. For days I've been so excited about starting school. I was looking forward to all the wonderful and fun things. But now that it starts tomorrow... my stomach feels weird. I feel like my insides are jittery. I don't feel hungry even though hamburgers are my favourite food. I feel scared, Papa."

Papa put his arm around Avery and held her close. She felt comforted snuggled into his shoulder.

"I wish I was like you, Papa, and never felt scared." Papa looked at Avery and smiled.

"Now where did you ever get an idea like that? Of course I get scared. In fact, I'm very nervous right now about my first hockey game of the season coming up on Saturday."

Avery looked up at Papa. "You are?"

"Sure," answered Papa. "I'm starting this season with a new team. I won't know anybody. I'm also being put in a higher division this year. That means the players are faster, the shots on net are harder, and the game is just a lot rougher. It's not easy being a goalie."

Avery thought about it for a moment and asked, "Then why do you play hockey, Papa?"

"Come with me," responded Papa, as he took Avery by the hand and walked with her into the house and down to the laundry room where he kept his hockey bag full of equipment.

Papa rummaged through the bag and answered, "This is why," as he handed Avery a puck.

It wasn't a shiny, glittery, magical-looking puck. It was just a plain black, ordinary old puck with a few scratches and a chip or two taken out of it.
Avery studied the puck for a few moments, then looked at Papa with a confused expression on her face.

Papa continued, "When I was nine years old, I was watching Hockey Night in Canada one Saturday evening. The Toronto Maple Leafs were playing the Chicago Blackhawks. Tony Esposito was in the net for Chicago, and that was the night I decided to be a goalie just like him. I asked my parents if they would put me into hockey, and they did.

"On the night of my first game, I remember feeling just like you do now. It felt like there were butterflies in my tummy. My body was all jittery, and I had no appetite all day.

"As I skated out onto the ice and headed for my net, my legs felt so shaky. I was sure that everyone could notice my nervousness and fear.

"The beginning of the game was terrifying. I didn't know what to expect. But then something amazing happened. After a couple of minutes, I faced my very first shot on net. Can you guess what happened?"

Avery was looking at Papa with her eyes wide open and shook her head.

"I stopped the puck! I also stopped fourteen more shots on net that game, only letting in one goal. I realized after my first save that hockey is so much fun and my jitters instantly disappeared.

"At the end of the game, as we were skating off the ice, my coach handed me the game puck as a souvenir of my very first goalie experience. That is the puck you are holding right now.

"I keep it in my bag to remind me that it's ok to be nervous or scared before a game. Because when you have faith in yourself and know you can do anything you set your mind to, you will get through it."

Papa told Avery to keep the puck inside her school backpack as a reminder that she had nothing to be worried or scared about.

"Papa, I feel so much better now that I have talked to you about this. It is very difficult to keep something that is bothering me to myself," Avery said, with a relieved tone in her voice and a happier spark in her eyes.

The next morning, Avery and her mom walked hand in hand to school. Avery clutched the shoulder strap of her backpack with her other hand.
The schoolyard was extremely busy with students and their parents walking around everywhere to find their teachers and classrooms.

Avery's mom said, "Let's try to find your teacher among all this crowd."

Avery noticed some other children with very worried and even scared looks on their faces. Avery started to feel jittery again.

She took her backpack off and unzipped it just enough so she could reach her hand in and feel around for the puck. As she located the hard rubber disk at the bottom of her bag, she felt a flood of relaxation and comfort rush through her body and mind.

WELCOME
BACK TO
SCHOOL

She said to herself, "I will get through this. I will be fine."

Finally, Mom saw a teacher standing near a tree. This lady was surrounded by a crowd of parents. She was talking to them with the brightest, most welcoming smile. She was holding a sign up with one hand that read, "Miss Paletta / Room 108."

WELCOME
MISS
PALETTA
ROOM 108

Avery and Mom introduced themselves while Miss Paletta crouched down to be eye to eye with Avery as she shook Avery's hand and welcomed her to school.

Mom gave Avery a kiss goodbye, but Avery noticed a tear in Mom's eye.

"It's ok, Mom," assured Avery. "I have a little something in my backpack that tells me I'm going to have a great day."

And with that, she gave Mom a big squishy hug and found her place in line to go into the school.

The children of Room 108 sat on the big, thick carpet with their legs crossed, hands in their laps, and all eyes and ears on Miss Paletta as she sat in a rocking chair at the front.

"Good morning class," Miss Paletta began. "I can already see that we are going to have a great year together."

Her voice was very soft and soothing. Avery knew she was going to be an awesome teacher.

Miss Paletta continued, "I feel a lot more relaxed now that I can see all your warm and friendly faces. I will admit, I have felt very nervous and jittery since yesterday."

A little girl named Lyla, who was sitting next to Avery, quietly raised her hand.

"Yes, Lyla. Do you have something to share?" inquired Miss Paletta.

Lyla asked, "Why were you feeling scared? You are a grown-up."

2+3

Miss Paletta responded, "Many people don't know that even teachers get nervous about the first day of school. We worry about our alarm clock not waking us up in time. We think about having to learn and remember all your names. We stress about putting a student on the wrong bus after school and many more things too.

I can see from some faces here that we have a little bit of first-day jitters as well. Let's just all relax, get to know one another, and have some fun today."
All the students were then excused from the carpet to go and explore the classroom.

Avery went to the painting easel. After some time there, she took her little painting over to Miss Paletta and said, "This is for you. I want you to keep it at your desk to remind you that you are a wonderful teacher and that we love you."

Miss Paletta looked at the painting, which was just a black circle in the middle of the page.

"Thank you, Avery. Can you tell me a bit about this painting?" asked Miss Paletta.

Avery responded, "It's a hockey puck."

Miss Paletta gave Avery a warm smile and said, "I think I understand. A long time ago, my grandma gave me a tennis ball that I always keep in my purse. I will look at this every morning when I come in."

She taped the painting to the side of her desk.

That evening during dinner, Avery could not stop talking to her parents about her first day at school.

She told them about the toys in the classroom, her spot on the carpet, her three new best friends, how they all must stand straight and tall during "Oh Canada," and of course, her most amazing teacher.

"My goodness, you had quite a fun-filled day today! But you might want to take some bites of your dinner before it gets cold," laughed Mom.

Dad said, "I'm glad to see you have that happy spark back in you."

Avery responded, "New things can be scary sometimes, even for big people, but I learned that talking with someone about it helps a lot."

That following Saturday night, Avery and her parents went to the arena to watch Papa's first hockey game of the season. They sat in the seats right behind the net so Papa would know he had his family right behind him.

As the players entered onto the ice, Papa skated a couple of laps around the rink to warm up. Then, as he approached his net, he looked up to see something that instantly took away his jitters.

A little girl with a beautiful bright smile... holding up a hockey puck.

THE END

9 7 9 8 8 8 9 7 9 5 7 1 1 8